Desert Critter Friends

Campout Capers

Mona Gansberg Hodgson
Illustrated by Chris Sharp

CPH
SAINT LOUIS

Dedicated with much love to John and Paula, Dan and Jeanine, and Jim and Karen—our camping buddies.

Desert Critter Friends Series

Friendly Differences

Thorny Treasures

Sour Snacks

Smelly Tales

Clubhouse Surprises

Desert Detectives

Jumping Jokers

Campout Capers

All Scripture quotations are taken from the HOLY BIBLE, NEW INTERNATIONAL VERSION®. NIV®. Copyright © 1973, 1978, 1984 by International Bible Society. Used by permission of Zondervan Publishing House. All rights reserved.

Text copyright © 1999 Mona Gansberg Hodgson

Published by Concordia Publishing House
3558 S. Jefferson Avenue, St. Louis, MO 63118-3968
Manufactured in the United States of America

Library of Congress Cataloging-in-Publication Data

Hodgson, Mona Gansberg, 1954–
    Campout capers / Mona Gansberg Hodgson ; illustrated by Chris Sharp.
      p.   cm. — (Desert critter friends series ; bk 8)
    Summary: On a camping trip, Jill the ground squirrel learns to handle her fear when she realizes that she can trust her nocturnal friends to help her.
    ISBN: 0-570-05482-6
    [1. Ground squirrels—Fiction. 2. Squirrels—Fiction. 3. Desert animals—Fiction. 4. Fear of the dark—Fiction. 5. Christian life—Fiction.] I. Sharp, Chris, 1954- ill. II. Title. III. Series: Hodgson, Mona Gansberg, 1954– Desert critter friends ; bk. 8.
PZ7.H6649Cam   1999
[E]—dc21   98-54210

1 2 3 4 5 6 7 8 9 10   08 07 06 05 04 03 02 01 00 99

Jill, the ground squirrel, put a flashlight in her bag. Then she checked her list.

Journal. Pencil. Flashlight. Jill tossed another pencil into her bag. She liked to write in her journal. And the desert critter friends' campout might give her a lot to write about.

Jill took a sip of her prickly pear juice. Just then she heard Lenny, the pack rat, calling her.

"Jill!" Lenny called.

Jill darted to her front door. "Come in."

Lenny scurried into Jill's rock home.

Rosie, the skunk, strolled in behind Lenny. "ACHOO! ACHOO!" Rosie sneezed. "Are you ready for the campout?"

"I guess so." Jill sighed before taking a last sip of her juice.

"You don't sound very ready," Lenny said.

Lenny scratched his furry white throat. "Are you still afraid to be out in the dark?"

"I'm not nocturnal (*knock-turn-all*) like you two are." Jill yawned. "You're used to being out and about at night. I'm not."

Rosie patted her friend on the
arm. "You don't have to be afraid.
We'll all be together. And you can
trust us to help you."

Lenny turned toward Rosie.
"Did I tell you I saw Quincy this
week? He said he's coming to the
campout."

Jill pulled her curtains closed.
"Who's Quincy?"

"Quincy's an artist who is nocturnal." Lenny scratched his fuzzy white throat.

"He usually keeps to himself," Rosie said.

"I'm still nervous about being out all night. But ..." Jill swung her bag over her shoulder, "since you're going to be with me, I think I'm ready to go to the clubhouse now."

The three desert critter friends scurried out Jill's door. Jill's tail curled up over her back as she followed Lenny and Rosie up a hill. Suddenly she stopped.

"I found something!" Jill called to her friends.

Rosie and Lenny stopped to see what Jill had found. Jill held up a white pointy stick with a black tip on it.

Lenny wiggled his nose. "Quincy's been here."

Jill wondered if the strange stick was an artist's tool. Maybe it was a paintbrush. She tucked it into her bag. Jill curled her tail up over her back and hurried up the hill to join Lenny and Rosie.

When the three friends arrived at the clubhouse, Jill looked all around. Bert, the roadrunner, loaded bags into a red wagon. Myra, the quail, packed food into it. Fergus, the owl, fluttered near Bert and Myra. Jill didn't see anyone new.

Quincy wasn't there yet.

Jill watched Toby and Wanda,
the cottontail rabbits, hop up.
Jamal, the jackrabbit, jumped
behind them. Taylor, the tortoise,
and Nadine, the javelina, strolled
behind them.

Jill carried her bag over to the
red wagon.

"Hey there, Jill." Bert took Jill's bag and put it in the wagon.

Just then Fergus flew over with a camera around his neck. "My camera will give us instant pictures of the campout capers."

"What's a *cay-purr*?" Rosie asked.

Jill yawned. "A *caper* is an adventure."

Fergus landed on a branch
in his clubhouse tree. The owl
hooted. "*WHO! WHO!*" Then he
cleared his throat. "Who hasn't put
their bag in Bert's wagon?"

Jamal jumped up and down. "He doesn't have my bag yet!" Jamal hopped over to Bert.

When Bert grabbed the handles on Jamal's bag, an alarm went off. It surprised Bert. He jumped and fluttered in the air.

"*HO! HO! HO!*" Jamal laughed.

Rosie smiled at Jill. "Looks like the campout capers have already begun."

nocturnal critters

"*WHO! WHO!*" Fergus cleared his throat again. "*WHO*ever is nocturnal will line up in front of the bookshelf. Those of you who are diurnal (*di-ur-nal*) and like to stay awake all day can pick one of us to be your camping buddy. Your

diurnal critters

buddy will help you learn about desert nightlife."

Fergus, Lenny, Rosie, and Nadine took their place in front of the bookshelf. They were all nocturnal.

Bert zoomed over to Lenny. Jill scurried over to Rosie. Toby and Wanda hopped over to Nadine. Myra scooted over to Rosie and Jill. Taylor strolled over to Fergus. And Jamal jumped up to Lenny and Bert.

ZOOM! Pulling the wagon behind him, Bert zoomed out in front of his friends. "Follow me to the campground!" *ZOOM!*

Jill and Myra and their camping buddy, Rosie, followed Bert through the desert. The other desert critters followed him too.

SCREECH! Bert stopped near the Verde River. "This is our campground!"

The critters all stopped.

21

Jill looked around. She liked having rocks to climb. But it was getting dark. She didn't like that. She started to feel afraid.

Rosie raised her arms to cover her mouth. *"ACHOO!"*

Just then Jill saw something scary in front of the rocks. "A MONSTER!" she screamed.

"HO! HO! HEE!" Rosie laughed. "That was no monster! That was me, your camping buddy!" She waved her arms. "You saw my shadow."

"Sorry." Jill said. "I'm trying not to be afraid, but being out during the night is so different. I need my flashlight."

Fergus flew over to Jill. "You
don't have to be afraid, Jill. You
can trust me to help you. I see
really well and I'm using my big
eyes to watch out for you."

TUG! TUG! TUG! Jill
pulled her flashlight out of her
bag. She shined the light on a ring
of rocks and a pile of firewood.

Bert zoomed up with a bucket
over his wing. "I'll get water for our
fire."

"Water?" Jill asked. "Water puts out a fire!"

"That's the whole idea." Taylor held his book under Jill's flashlight. "My camping safety book says to build a ring with something that won't burn." Taylor pushed his glasses up on his nose. "It also says to have water nearby to put the fire out."

ZOOM! Bert set the water bucket next to the rock ring.

Taylor turned a page in his book. "We need a shovel to help us pile dirt on the campfire before we leave. We don't want to start a desert fire."

"No problem!" Jamal stood up on his front feet. "I take my shovels with me wherever I go!" He waved his two big back feet in the air. Then he laughed. *"HO! HO! HO!"*

All the desert critters laughed with him.

Jill helped Rosie pour a glass of juice for everyone. Wanda and Toby helped Myra put mesquite bean pods on sticks. Fergus took pictures of the desert critter friends working together.

"I have an idea!" Rosie clapped her fuzzy paws together. "Let's make shadow puppets." She strolled over between the campfire and some big rocks. "First, make sure you have light behind you." Suddenly Rosie faked a loud sneeze. "*ACHOO!*" She raised her arms. "Look. I'm Jill's monster!"

Jill laughed so hard she spilled her juice.

Camping out in the dark still made Jill nervous, but she liked being with her friends. She peeked up at the night sky. Stars twinkled. The moon glowed. Suddenly the

way her nocturnal friends lived
didn't seem so scary. Just different.

Jill stood up on her back feet
and looked around. She wondered
when Quincy would show up.

ZOOM! Bert zoomed in front of the rocks. "I want to try making a shadow puppet!" He spread his wings. "Look!" he called, flapping his wings. "I'm an eagle!"

"HO! HO! HO!" Jamal laughed. "Well ... not exactly."

"HA! HA! HA!" Bert laughed.

FLASH! Fergus took a picture of the desert critter friends having fun together.

Taylor pushed his glasses up on his nose. "This time, Fergus, I'll take a picture with you in it."

Fergus flew over to Taylor and hung the camera over the tortoise's neck. Then Fergus landed on a low branch near the other critters.

Jill munched on a bean pod as she watched Taylor. He strolled away to find a good spot to take a picture.

Suddenly the camera went flying into the air. And something tumbled over Taylor. Jill blinked. The thing that had tumbled over Taylor was coming right at her!

Suddenly Jill yelled. *"YEOW!"*
Whatever it was ... it poked her.
She remembered what her friends
had said and she tried not to be
afraid. Jill stood up on her back feet
and rubbed her tummy.

A bright flash lit up a strange
looking critter standing right in
front of her. He had lots of white
and black sticks all over his body.
The kind of stick Jill had found on
the hill.

Bert grabbed the camera before
it hit the ground.

Lenny scurried over to Jill. He chuckled. "You just met Quincy. And I think Taylor got a picture of it. Quincy's a porcupine."

Quincy didn't look like anything Jill had ever seen. He looked like he had paintbrushes sticking out all over him. "You're Quincy?"

"Yes." Quincy, the porcupine, backed away from Jill. "Sorry I poked you with my quills. I don't see very well."

Jamal jumped up and down. "I have a joke!" He laughed.

All the desert critter friends gathered around the jackrabbit.

Jamal cleared his throat and looked at Jill. "What do you get when a porcupine takes a ride on a tortoise?"

Jill scratched her tummy.

"A SLOWPOKE!" Jamal jumped and laughed. "*HO! HO! HO!*"

40

"HO! HEE! HEE!" Jill laughed.

"A SLOWPOKE! That's a good one!" Taylor laughed. *"HEE! HEE! HO!"*

Soon all the critters were laughing. Jill was writing in her journal. She didn't want to forget any of the campout capers or what she had learned about trusting her friends. If she had given in to her fear and stayed home, she would have missed the campout fun. When she was afraid, she could trust her friends to stay with her and help her.

God cares about you! He loves you so much that He sent His Son to die for you. When you are afraid, God will help you. You can always trust Him to take care of you.

Trust in the Lord with all your heart. Proverbs 3:5

Hi kids!

These words from Jill's journal are written in the Hebrew way, from right to left. Write the words on the lines in the English way to find out what God promises.

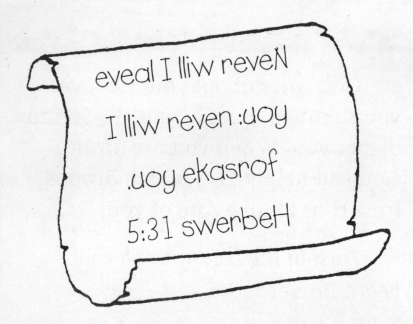

eveal I lliw reveN

I lliw reven :uoy

.uoy ekasrof

5:31 swerbeH

For Parents and Teachers:

We've all felt the fear of the unknown. Like Jill, we've been afraid to leave our comfort zone to experience something new. We may have even viewed differences in people as frightening.

At one time or another, all kids struggle with fear. Fear of darkness. Fear of moving to a new place, meeting new people, being left alone. Fear of failure at school. Fear of changing life situations because of divorce or death ...

The psalm writer David knew quite a bit about fear. Whether facing a lion, a bear, or a giant, he knew that God was in control. He proclaimed, "When I am afraid, I will trust in You" (Psalm 56:4).

Our kids live in an alarming world. They face real dangers and need to be taught how to avoid them and how to cope with them. But kids also need to know that God is in control. That's why God's promise from Hebrews 13:5 was chosen for this story's activity. "Never will I leave you. Never will I forsake you."

Because of what Jesus Christ did for us on the cross, we face no real or imagined danger alone. God is at our side, cloaking us in His matchless love. He fills us with strength and trust. God will never leave us or fail us.

In Psalm 20:7, David says, "Some trust in chariots and some in horses, but we trust in the name of the LORD our God." In what, or in whom, do the kids in our care trust? In what, or in whom, do we place our trust? God draws us to Himself through His Son and gives us the faith to trust Him.

Here are some questions and activities you can use as discussion starters to help your children understand these concepts.

Discussion Starters

1. What were the desert critters going to do in this story?

2. Have you ever been camping? Did you enjoy it? Did anything scary happen?

3. Why was Jill afraid to go camping?

4. What did Jill do when she was afraid?

5. Have you ever been afraid? What did you do when you were afraid?

6. Read Hebrews 13:6 together. Who will help you when you are afraid?

7. What would you say to a friend who was afraid? What would you say about God's love?

Pray together. Thank God for loving you so much that He sent His Son to be your Savior. Thank Him for helping you to trust Him. Ask God to show you how to help others when they are afraid.

What will you do the next time you are afraid? Tell me on these lines.

_____

_____

_____

_____